# THE IMMORTAL PEACH TREE

JADE EMPEROR

FENGHUANG

Also available in the
Brownstone's Mythical Collection

*Arthur and the Golden Rope*
*Marcy and the Riddle of the Sphinx*

*Brownstone's Mythical Collection: Kai and the Monkey King* © Flying Eye Books 2019

First edition published in 2019 by Flying Eye Books, an imprint
of Nobrow Ltd. 27 Westgate Street, London E8 3RL.

Text and illustrations © Joe Todd-Stanton 2019.
Joe Todd-Stanton has asserted his right under the Copyright, Designs
and Patents Act, 1988, to be identified as the Author and Illustrator of this Work.

1 3 5 7 9 10 8 6 4 2

Published in the US by Nobrow (US) Inc.
Printed in Poland on FSC certified paper.

MIX
Paper from
responsible sources
FSC® C001693
FSC
www.fsc.org

ISBN: 978-1-83874-024-5
www.flyingeyebooks.com

-JOE TODD-STANTON-

BROWNSTONE'S MYTHICAL COLLECTION

# KAI and the MONKEY KING

FLYING EYE BOOKS
London | New York

Hello dear reader — long time, no see!

Welcome to the depths of the Brownstone family vault. To the untrained eye, it may merely look like an absurd assortment of the macabre, but to me every object is a chance to understand the story of my mysterious family.

This is one of the most important objects of all. The Brownstone Family Tree.

After Arthur and Marcy, the Brownstone family grew and grew, then spread to every corner of the globe.

THE BROWNSTONE FAMILY TREE

Their mission:

"To collect and protect mythological artefacts and creatures."

When I look at this, so many adventures and wonderful artefacts spring to mind that it's hard to decide which one to speak of next...

OMNIUM RERUM PRINCIPIA PARVA SUNT

I could tell you the tale of the five-coloured dragon neck jewels...
or perhaps the quest for the flaming sword of the Bird Prince?

Maybe the journey to rescue the hidden treasure from the three
Rhein Maidens ... or even the legend of the dastardly Cactus Cat?

But no, today only one tale is so fantastical and intriguing to me that I cannot keep it to myself any longer... It's the story of how this small and humble peach pit came into my possession.

This is the adventure of two Brownstones. A daring daughter named Kai and her patient mother named Wen.

Wen travelled from land to land on her quest as a Brownstone, with Kai always by her side. Kai was constantly learning from her mum how to observe, document and contain the mythical phenomena they came across.

But as Kai got older, she often grew bored. She yearned for a challenge with more danger and excitement.

The news of their skills spread far and wide, until one day they received a letter from a village requesting their assistance.

"Once a year we are attacked by a terrible beast who destroys everything in its path! Can you please help us?"

Wen knew this was a much more dangerous task than any Kai had assisted her with before, but she also knew that, as Brownstones, they had to help.

Wen reluctantly agreed to the task and took Kai straight to the village library. She knew there would be a clue to defeating the beast hidden somewhere within its shelves.

As the day wore on, Wen became more and more focused on the task...

...and Kai grew more and more bored.

She couldn't believe it. They finally found the challenge she'd been waiting for and they were just sitting around reading old books?!

Frustrated, Kai rummaged through the library's shelves until she found a book that looked like it could be useful. Maybe if Kai brought this back, her mum would let her be more involved in the task.

She struggled to contain her excitement...

...and got a little bit carried away.

Exasperated and tired, Wen lost her patience. As punishment, she banished Kai to the other side of library, so she could finally work in peace.

Angry, hurt and alone Kai ventured deeper and deeper into the library.

Until an ancient scroll peeking out from behind a cobwebbed bookshelf caught her eye.

Born from a magic stone sat atop a mountain, Sūn Wùkōng started life with the regular monkeys, though it was clear he was different. He soon became bored and longed for excitement. So he decided to push himself to see what he was made of.

First, he trained in combat and agility until he became so skilled that he was declared the Monkey King.

Next, he took on the dragons of the four seas. By defeating them he acquired enchanted garments and cloud-walking boots. He soon felt invincible!

Finally, he travelled to the East Sea and took a magical golden staff from the Dragon King, Ao Guăng. This provided him with immense power.

But the Monkey King wanted more, and he soon set his sights on the heavenly palace of the Jade Emperor. The Emperor's garden contained magical peaches, each of which added 3,000 years to the life of anyone who ate one. With enough of these, he could become immortal.

The Monkey King found the peaches and started to eat them, hoping to gain immortality. But before he could eat enough, he was foiled by the Jade Emperor. The Emperor thought that the Monkey King was far too inconsiderate and reckless for such power.

The two of them went to war, and a long battle commenced. Finally, the Emperor — with the help of the Heavenly Army and Buddha — defeated the Monkey King.

They punished him by imprisoning him inside the Buddha Palm, buried deep in the mountains. It is there he will remain unless a great and powerful adventurer can break the golden seal and free him.

After reading the scroll, Kai quickly made up her mind. She already knew she was a great adventurer and if her mum wouldn't listen to her, she would take on the beast with the help of the Monkey King instead!

Kai took some supplies and the scroll, then snuck away — ready to start her first adventure without her mum holding her back.

After a long and tiring trek through the mountains, Kai finally reached the Buddha Palm. Trapped inside, just as the scroll had said, was the Monkey King.

Hello great Monkey King. Please tell me, if I break the golden seal and free you from the Buddha Palm, will you help me defeat a monster?

Will I help you defeat a monster?! I can defeat anything I WANT! I am the Monkey King, the greatest warrior the world has ever known! I have bathed in the energies of Earth and Heaven, I know the Way of the Seventy-Two Transformations and I can travel a thousand miles in one somersault. There is NOTHING I cannot defeat.

So sure, I will help you. But first, you must retrieve my staff from the mighty Dragon King under the ocean, then break the golden seal. It's a simple mission that any powerful adventurer could do in their sleep...

So Kai, ready for the challenge, went to collect the staff...

It wasn't quite as simple as the Monkey King had said...

...but years of adventuring with her mum had prepared her for the task.

Triumphant, Kai returned to the Buddha Palm and smashed the seal with all her might.

Once free, the Monkey King told Kai that before he could help her, he had some unfinished business of his own to take care of.

Before Kai had time to take in what had happened, the two of them were soaring through the sky towards the palace of the Jade Emperor...

...and Kai had never had so much fun in her life!

As they approached the back walls of the
Emperor's garden, Kai was still lost in wonder.

But as soon as they landed, she felt like this might not be as easy as it
first seemed ... and she really needed to get back to help her mum.

The Monkey King told her not to worry. He promised that all he
needed was a pile of peaches from the garden. Just one big pile
of ripe peaches, and then they would go and help Kai's mum.

Kai tiptoed around the garden, carefully collecting the peaches for the Monkey King.

Unfortunately, the Monkey King had other ideas...

...he soon grew restless...

...and got a little bit carried away.

Suddenly, the garden sprang to life!

With the Monkey King nowhere in sight ... Kai had no choice but to RUN!

At the last moment, he finally came to her rescue...

...though by then, it was already too late.

When the Monkey King realised Kai only had one peach left,
he demanded that they return to the Emperor's palace to get more.

Kai refused to go back without defeating the beast
first and the Monkey King refused to help Kai stop
the beast without getting more peaches.

And so, Kai was angry, hurt and alone once again.

She made her way back to her mum, still clutching the one squashed peach she managed to save. It was all she had to show for her daring adventures.

As she got closer to the village, she saw a terrifying sight.

The gigantic beast was stalking down from the mountains and the only thing standing in its path was the tiny, helpless figure of Kai's mum!

Kai and her mum had taken on every challenge together, and she wasn't going to let this one be any different.

She mustered all the strength she had left and sprinted down the mountain...

...but the beast saw her coming and quickly moved to block her.

Its rotten breath hit Kai in the face as it revealed its giant jaws, ready to swallow her whole!

Then all of a sudden, a bolt of bright light hit the creature square in the face!

The beast recoiled in fear as a dozen more explosions flashed across the sky. It must be the Monkey King with his magic staff, thought Kai. He had returned to keep his promise!

She swung around to see...

45

...her mum!

She beamed with pride and awe.

And as the sky lit up with fireworks, the beast retreated
back to the mountains and Kai ran into her mum's arms.

Wen apologised for losing her patience and asked Kai never to run off like that again. Then she showed Kai the book that was key to defeating the beast.

Kai couldn't believe it — it was the one that she had found!

Kai apologised too, and told Wen all about her adventure, showing her the squashed peach. Then it was Wen's turn to beam with pride and awe.

Once all the action was over, Wen and Kai gave the book and the fireworks to the villagers, so they would always be safe from the beast.

The pair then continued on their travels, ready to take on their next great adventure — whatever it might be.

And once a year, for the next thousand years, a daring daughter named Kai and her patient mother named Wen, returned to the village to watch the fireworks.

And that is the tale of Kai, the Monkey King and this humble peach — well what's left of it anyway. And what happened to the Monkey King, I hear you ask? Did he return to battle the Jade Emperor? Did he manage to become immortal? Well, I guess that's another story, for another time...